Seek the Mermaid's
Magic in your Heart!
CAO
Joy to you!
Jan DiRuzzo

The Lost Mermaid

A Shem Creek Moonlight Jamboree

Dedicated to
Collyn
My inspiration for storytelling

Nathan
The newest reader to join our family

Our precious nieces and nephews
near and abroad

and

Thank You Sweet Elves
(you know who you are)

Revised Edition July 2014
Copyright 2009 Text: Jan DiRuzzo
Copyright 2009 Illustrations: Dave Sullins

ISBN 978-0-9832344-0-1
Library of Congress control number 2011923276
Printed in China

Visit www.TheLostMermaid.com to order additional copies.

The Lost Mermaid

A Shem Creek Moonlight Jamboree

Written by

Jan DiRuzzo

Illustrated by

Dave Sullins

Graphics Editor

Joe DiRuzzo

Dream Maker Publications

Charleston, South Carolina

On a creek called Shem,
down the beach and around the bend
sat a lonely little mermaid upon a glistening throne,
carved by the sea from rainbow-colored stone.

Lily
was the name her friends called her before,
but no one ever called her Lily anymore.
No one ever asked Lily
to play games that were sweet and silly.
She was so sad and lonely.
She wished someone would say,
"Will you play with me today?"

Lily had been born with vanilla-colored curls
and was her mother's only little girl.
Her mom named her Lily after she had seen
a vanilla-colored water lily, floating on a pond —
"the perfect crown," she thought,
"made for my little queen."

She had lived with her mother, father, friends
and brother, Finn,

in a place far away
from the creek called Shem,
down the beach
and around the bend

in pink crystal caves beneath the sea,
surrounded by fan coral fences and anemones,
all laced in raspberry, lavender, and green.

Oh, life beneath the sea had been very serene....

Until

One day, a big, blustery storm came along
that foamed and frothed and churned up the sea,
and tossed and turned Lily,
separating her from friends, her home and her family.

So now poor Lily sat alone.
so sad, missing her family and her home.

Each day when the crabs left the sea,
passing her by on their way to the beach,
she would wave to them and say,
"Excuse me! Excuse me!
Has anyone seen my mother, father, friends
or brother, Finn, today?"

The crabs, ever so shy,
would quickly close their eyes,
sink into the sand, and there they'd stay,
leaving a tearful Lily to pine away.

Early one morning, Lily floated by
a family of oysters with sleepy looking eyes.

All snuggled and cozy in their beds,
she smiled at the oysters, waved her arms, and said,
"Has anyone seen my mother, father, friends
or brother, Finn, today?"
The oysters sank into their muddy beds,
slammed their shells, and there they stayed.
Not one little oyster talked to Lily that day.

About noon, a school of fish swam by.

Lily blinked and rubbed her eyes.
"Could it be? Could it be my family?"
She leapt from her throne into the sea.
"Yes, this must be my family!"

The little fish scattered in a terrible fright.

They had never seen such an odd-looking sight.

Suddenly, there she was again
left frightened and alone.
She began to cry, feeling so sad,
missing her family and her home.
Quickly she propelled her fin,
and returned to her throne—
alone once again.

You see

The crabs, the oysters and the fish
were afraid of Lily.
They were all confused
by the language that she used.
She didn't look like the other oysters
or crabs or fish.

Oh No!!

They had all seen whales and dolphins
and sharks and shrimp,

but never, **never** a fish that looked
like this.

Then one moonlit night
while poor Lily slept
alone on her throne,
the noble seahorses
from the distant
reaches of Edisto
and Folly Beaches
came riding in
   to the creek
      called Shem
         down the beach
            and around the bend.

Riding high across
white-capped seas,
they came to decree
The Shem Creek
Moonlight
Jamboree.

Oh! It was a magical night!
Fish even flew on dragonfly wings
under the moon's silvery light.

Sea friends near and far came to celebrate this season.
Why, there was music and dancing and hundreds of reasons
for thousands of fireflies to explode into fusion
like fireworks spraying the sky with sparkling illusions.
There were fountains
glistening in greens,
pink tambourines,
and cherry tart stars!

Even the Loggerhead family
made their turtle debut.
Mama, Papa and Baby Lou
left the Sanctuary of their sleepy dune.
Waddling across tranquil beaches on Kiawah Isle,

they followed an old family map for many a mile.
They crept past alligators snoozing beneath the pine,
and thought, "We'll not be the evening meal on which they'll dine."

At last they reached the point on the beach
where the currents would carry
them straight to Shem Creek.

Slipping quietly into the sea,

they swam like winged angels
beneath the waves,

and reached the Jamboree
in just a few days.

When the Loggerheads arrived,
    the crowd went Wild!

Then Papa lent his big, brown shell
to those calypso drum sounds
that Mama and Lou
could play so well.

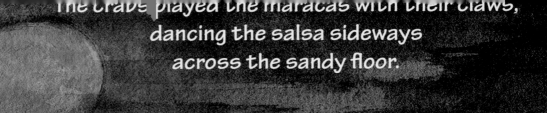

The crabs played the maracas with their claws,
dancing the salsa sideways
across the sandy floor.

The oyster band hummed the Cha Cha Cha,
squishing water from the squishy shore.

The seahorses swayed
at the edge of the beach,
tapping their tails
in two-beat harmony.

But the funniest sight to see
was Bobby the Blowfish
with bulging eyes and puffy cheeks,
blowing tunes to the moonlight jamboree!

The dolphins, too, hit the silvery stage.
Mama, Papa, and Baby Dawn
swam in from the Isle of Palm.

Papa led the Tango Tail Dance
while Mama and Dawn followed along —
spinning to the left — spinning to the right —
Ooh la la! What a vision! What a night!

The Moonlight Jamboree was in full swing,
and poor Lily still slept
alone on her throne.

Then much to the stars' surprise,
the Man-in-the-Moon winked a smiling eye
on the little mermaid asleep under the starlit sky.

Instantly, she awoke with a jolt.
"I hear sounds!
Why there's clapping and tapping."
She thought, "Is this a dream, or have I been found?"

She often dreamt about the evening meal
when mother, father and brother, Finn,
would play the sea fiddle and mandolin.
Lily and Finn would dance and sing,
celebrating birthdays, holidays,
and all sorts of fun things.

But the music played on, and Lily thought, "Wait!

I'm not dreaming; I'm awake!"

Memories of her family stirred in her heart.
And though she was afraid because it was dark,
she leapt from her throne into the sea,
and swam as fast as she could
toward that sweet memory.

She followed the sounds
along the creek called Shem,
down the beach and
around the bend.

Then gazing up to the sky she saw
diamonds and fountains and stars galore.

Lily swished onto the stage of the Jamboree
where everyone was playing and dancing in harmony.

Well, she swam right up to those seahorses,
tapping and swaying to those calypso beats
and said, "Pardon me, I am Lily,
and I am looking for my family.
Has anyone seen anyone who looks like me?"

Much to her surprise, the seahorses didn't run away
like all the other creatures she had met that day.
They were not at all confused
by the language that she used.

In fact,
they answered her
by name
in a language
that was
the same.

Sammy, the Seahorse
was the first to speak.
He said, "Lily, I had always hoped
one day we'd meet.

"Yes, I know who you and your family are.
The mermaids and the mermen
live in a deep watery kingdom
beneath a bright raspberry star.

"My name is Sammy, the Seahorse,
and I am a distant cousin of yours.
I have heard that you were lost."

All at once, the music stopped!

The crabs, the oysters, dolphins and fish
had spied Lily, and they began to scatter.
"Hey," said Sammy, "Hold on! What's the matter?
Don't be afraid of Lily here.
Believe me when I tell you, you have nothing to fear.

"I know that you have never seen
a fish that looks like this.
But trust me when I say,
she has many special gifts.
You will not be sorry if you let her stay
to sing and play with us today."

The sea friends began to grumble and debate.
"Should she go or should she stay?
No, no her differences are just too great.
Whoever heard of a fish anywhere —

with **hair!!**"

Then frantically, Sammy screamed,
"Friends, friends, it's too late!
Our lives are at stake!

Run! Run! Run while you can!"
They all looked up at the dark gray fin
slicing through the sea mist,
bearing down on all of them.

It was a giant, gray shark. His mouth gaped
like the opening to a huge, black cave.

His teeth, jagged like a saber saw blade,
glared in the icy light.

His eyes, dark, beady, and mean
were staring down at the meal
on which he had set his sight.

As he grew near,
the sea friends froze in fear.

At once, he was upon them,
his teeth dripping,
ready to rip up and chew
Sammy the Seahorse,
Bobby the Blowfish,
and Baby Lou.

Suddenly, out of the blue,
Lily did the most unusual thing.
She didn't flee.
She didn't flinch.
She didn't move an inch.

Do you know what she did?

She began to sing a magical song
and the night air sweetened and rippled
with the tinkling of bells and crystal.

And then —
THERE WAS A MIRACLE!!

The shark splashed and wiggled.
Then he rolled and giggled
as if someone had just tickled
his dorsal fin.

He began to smile;
he began to spin.

He became so spellbound,
he turned upside down
and floated belly-up
back into the deep, blue sea again.

The sea friends realized
that much to their surprise
they, too, wore great, big, happy smiles.
They had never felt such peace and joy
in their entire lives.

Sammy explained that Lily's songs
have magical sounds.
They make hunger and fear disappear,
while happiness abounds.

Lily had saved their lives.
They all felt very ashamed
for the mean way they had behaved.
They were sorry they had snubbed Lily
and ran away.

All at once, the sea friends
began to whistle and cheer!

Lily was so pleased
to see smiling faces so near.
Her eyes filled with happy tears.
She began to hum a playful song
that tickled the ear and tickled the tongue.

Her new friends
soared high in the air, then down,
shouting "Lily! Lily!" across sparkling waves and all around.

From that day forward,
her new friends vowed to be more accepting
of creatures like Lily that they had never met nor seen.
They celebrated Lily and made her the Queen
of the Shem Creek Moonlight Jamboree.
From that night on, Lily was never alone.
She had new friends who promised
         to help her find her family
                  and her home.

Glossary

Anemones are a group of plants that live under the sea. They are named after a flower and are closely related to jellyfish and coral.

Blowfish are closely related to the porcupine fish, which have large spines. They are small to medium in size and can inflate rapidly, expanding their bellies with water until they are almost completely round in shape.

Dolphins are marine mammals, closely related to whales and porpoises. They can range in size from 4 feet to 30 feet and are found mostly in shallow seas worldwide. Their species is about 10 million years old, and they are considered to be among the most intelligent of animals, often appearing friendly and playful.

Loggerhead Turtles live in oceans all over the world except in the coldest seas. An adult loggerhead is about 3 feet long and weighs on average about 250 pounds, but they can reach weights up to 800 pounds. Loggerheads that reach adulthood often live longer than 30 years, and some have lived more than 198 years. They face danger from pollution, trash in the oceans, and fishing nets and are threatened by human development in their nesting areas. They are at risk from boats when they swim near shore, sometimes being injured or killed when hit by boat propellers. All sea turtles are protected by the U.S. Endangered Species Act. Many individuals volunteer to help protect the loggerhead turtles. Check out www.follyturtles.com for volunteer opportunities in South Carolina, nationally, and internationally.

Oysters have hard shells and live in shallow water along a seacoast or river. Their shells provide places where other small animals can live. Hundreds of small animals, such as barnacles, mussels, and anemones make oyster reefs their home. A group of oysters together is called a bed.

Seahorses live in shallow, warm seas throughout the world. Their head and neck resemble a horse's head and neck, and their tail allows them to grasp items, such as sea grass or reef surfaces. They range in size from an inch to a foot long and can turn bright colors, depending upon their surroundings.

Places of Interest

Edisto Beach, a small coastal town, located on Edisto Island in Colleton County, SC, was originally inhabited by the Edistow Indians. Edisto Beach is a popular vacation destination with expansive beaches, camping, and fishing.

Folly Beach, a city in Charleston County, SC, located on historic Folly Island, is renowned for fishing, swimming, and surfing. Morris Island Lighthouse provides historic charm to Folly's coastal landscape. Completed in 1876, it is being preserved and restored. Folly Beach was originally inhabited by the Bohicket Indian tribe.

Isle of Palms, a city in Charleston County, SC, located on the barrier island of Isle of Palms, is a semi-tropical retreat. Bordered by beautiful beaches and containing a maze of marsh creeks, it is a great spot for shrimping, fishing, or crabbing. Isle of Palms was originally inhabited by the Sewee Indians.

Kiawah, a town in Charleston County, SC, located on the barrier island of Kiawah, has one of the oldest loggerhead turtle protection programs in the country. It is also a major US tourist site and home to the five-star Sanctuary Hotel as well as many other lovely hotels, beautiful beaches, and golfing. Kiawah was named for the Kiawah Indians.

Shem Creek was originally occupied by the Sewee Indians. Captain O'Sullivan, one of the early settlers to arrive from England in 1680, founded the areas now known as Mt. Pleasant and nearby Sullivan's Island, which bears his name. Today, Shem Creek is a highlight for the Charleston, SC boating, fishing, and seafood fans. Fresh seafood comes in daily from locally parked shrimp boats. Dolphins often follow the fish and shrimp boats into the creek to check out the daily catch.

About the Author

Jan DiRuzzo has had a lasting passion for literature and particularly fantasy. She loved reading and telling stories first to her younger sister, then her daughter, and now her young nephew, Collyn. She has always lived near the sea with her family and her favorite horse, Caleb, formerly in Newport, Rhode Island, and currently in the low country of South Carolina. While kayaking with the dolphins along Shem Creek, she became inspired by the diversity of life both on and off shore and has woven these themes together to share with other young readers.

About the Artist

Dave Sullins has been a painter and print maker for over 20 years. He has studied painting, drawing, and print making with modern day masters in Taos, New Mexico, at the University of New Mexico, and at the Belles Artes in San Miguel de Allende, Mexico. He is a resident of Taos, New Mexico and has his studio in the nearby town of Pilar on the Rio Grande. Dave is also a summer resident of Vancouver Island, Canada, residing in the west coast artist colony of Tahsis, British Columbia in the historic Nootka Sound area of Vancouver Island's scenic fiord region. Because of his cultural association with Mexico, Canada and the United States, he is known as The North American Artist. He paints still life in oil in the classical old-world style with a strong sense of light, and his water colors also reflect that vibrancy of light. He is available for commission work. Check out and enjoy his website at david@sullinsart.com.